BEFORE
I Was Your
MOTHER

WID.

Ourselves

BEFORE
I Was Your
MOTHER

Written by

KATHRYN LASKY

Illustrated by

LEUYEN PHAM

Voyager Books * Harcourt, Inc.

Orlando   Austin   New York

San Diego   Toronto   London

www.HarcourtBooks.com

First Voyager Books edition 2007

Voyager Books is a trademark of Harcourt, Inc., registered
in the United States of America and/or other jurisdictions.

The Library of Congress has cataloged the hardcover edition as follows:
Lasky, Kathryn.
Before I was your mother/Kathryn Lasky; illustrated by LeUyen Pham.
p. cm.
Summary: A mother tells her own daughter what she was like
and what she used to do when she was a little girl.
[1. Mothers and daughters—Fiction.   2. Mothers—Fiction.]
I. Pham, LeUyen, ill.   II. Title.
PZ7.L3274Bb 2003
[E]—dc21   2001007544
ISBN 978-0-15-201464-3
ISBN 978-0-15-205842-5 pb

H G F E D C B A

The illustrations in this book were done in watercolor, pen and ink,
and collage on Arches watercolor paper.
The display type was set in Worcester Round and Florens Flourished.
The text type was set in Minister Light.
Color separations by Bright Arts Ltd., Hong Kong
Manufactured by South China Printing Company, Ltd., China
Production supervision by Pascha Gerlinger
Designed by Lydia D'moch

For my mother, H. F. L., with love,
and for my daughter, M. G. K.,
who brings me joy

—K. L.

To LeHuong Pham,
before she was my mother

—L. P.

You know, I wasn't always your mother.

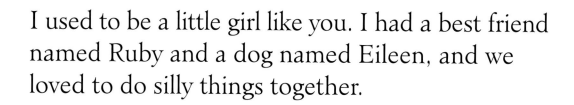

I used to be a little girl like you. I had a best friend named Ruby and a dog named Eileen, and we loved to do silly things together.

Once I dressed Eileen up in a tutu, and Ruby and I put on a circus in my backyard. Eileen was a lion, and Ruby and I were lion tamers.

I wasn't always your mother, who knows how to cook and to fix broken things.

Once I had legs that didn't reach the floor. I sat on a stool at the kitchen counter and ate my mother's sweet treats. She knew how to suspend fruit in Jell-O. I thought it was magic.

Once I broke the china cat into a million pieces, and my mother glued it back together perfectly. I couldn't even see the cracks.

I wasn't always your mother, who tells you to *shush* when I'm on the telephone or to *quiet down* when you and your friends get too wild.

Once I loved making lots of noise. I remember when Ruby and I put on hula skirts and roller-skated down the sidewalk, bellowing out a song as loud as we could.

And then there was the time—that starry, starry night—when we turned the garbage can lids upside down and tap-danced on them, just to hear the *rat-a-tat-tat* bounce into the darkness.

I wasn't always your mother, who carries a purse full of bills to pay and wears shoes that won't hurt my feet.

Once I was a little girl, who carried secret stuff in a green velvet bag and wanted a pair of bright red patent-leather shoes more than anything.

I wore my favorite cowboy boots to cousin Sylvia's wedding, and when my father bought me tall rubber boots, the kind firefighters wear, I wore mine to bed. I loved shoes—all kinds.

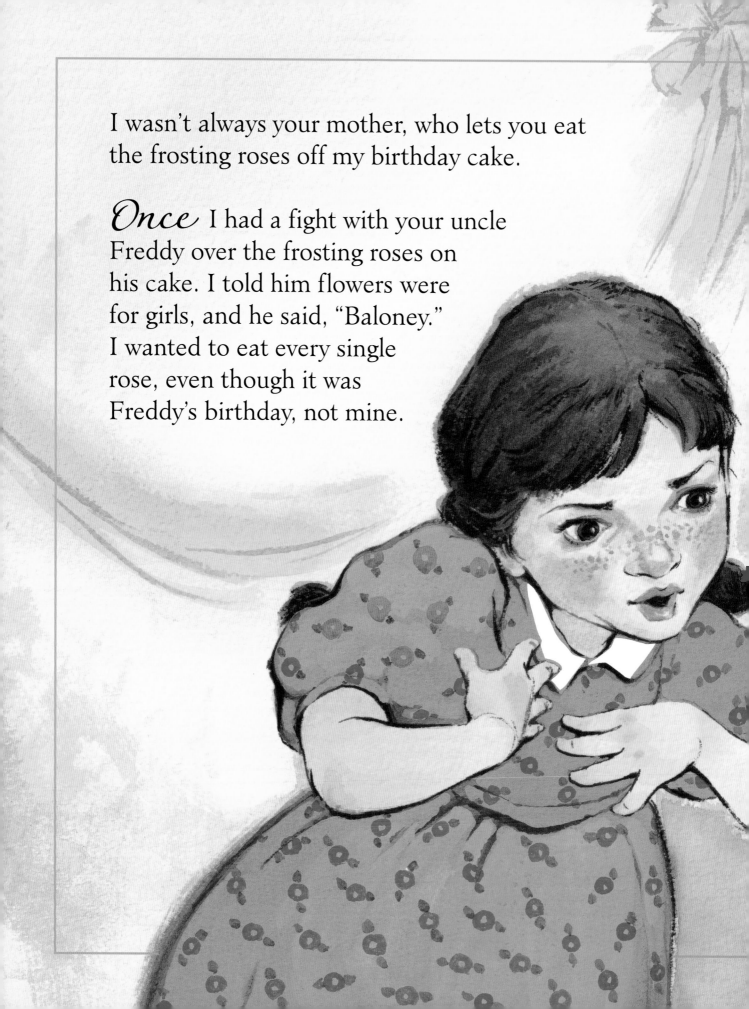

I wasn't always your mother, who lets you eat the frosting roses off my birthday cake.

Once I had a fight with your uncle Freddy over the frosting roses on his cake. I told him flowers were for girls, and he said, "Baloney." I wanted to eat every single rose, even though it was Freddy's birthday, not mine.

I wasn't always your mother, racing around with to-do lists in my hand and glasses sliding down my nose and pencils stuck in my hair.

Once I was a little girl with braids. Sometimes I wore stick-out party dresses and stood perfectly still in first position, with my arms just so, dreaming ballerina dreams.

But mostly I wore overalls with a special pocket for holding my special things. And I had a favorite tree with a hollow, where I left scribble-scrabble notes and bracelets strung with beads for my imaginary friend.

Before I was your mother, I had a doll I named Katie, and then I got a teddy bear I named Katie, and my fuzzy duck and velvet seal were named Katie, too. I tucked them in at night and read them stories. I made birthday cakes out of clay and gave my Katies all the frosting roses to eat.

Now I am your mother, and you are my only Katie.
I tuck you in and tell you stories about the time
before your time, when I was a little girl who ate
all the frosting roses, who slept in her firefighter
boots, who tap-danced on garbage can lids...

. . . and who dreamed of having
her own little girl to love.